TEN BIRDS

Meet a Monster

For Calder, Finley, Dave and Macaroni

Text and illustrations © 2013 Cybèle Young

All rights reserved. No part of this publication may be reproduced, stored in a retrieval system or transmitted, in any form or by any means, without the prior written permission of Kids Can Press Ltd. or, in case of photocopying or other reprographic copying, a license from The Canadian Copyright Licensing Agency (Access Copyright). For an Access Copyright license, visit www.accesscopyright.ca or call toll free to 1-800-893-5777.

Kids Can Press acknowledges the financial support of the Government of Ontario, through the Ontario Media Development Corporation's Ontario Book Initiative; the Ontario Arts Council; the Canada Council for the Arts; and the Government of Canada, through the CBF, for our publishing activity.

Published in Canada by	Published in the U.S. by
Kids Can Press Ltd.	Kids Can Press Ltd.
25 Dockside Drive	2250 Military Road
Toronto, ON M5A 0B5	Tonawanda, NY 14150

www.kidscanpress.com

The artwork in this book was rendered in pen and ink on paper. The text is set in Incognito.

Edited by Karen Li and Stacey Roderick
Designed by Karen Powers

This book is smyth sewn casebound.
Manufactured in Tseung Kwan O, NT Hong Kong, China, in 3/2013 by Paramount Printing Co. Ltd.

CM 13 0 9 8 7 6 5 4 3 2 1

LIBRARY AND ARCHIVES CANADA CATALOGUING IN PUBLICATION

YOUNG, CYBÈLE, 1972–
TEN BIRDS MEET A MONSTER / WRITTEN AND ILLUSTRATED BY CYBÈLE YOUNG.

(TEN BIRDS)
ISBN 978-1-55453-955-0

I. TITLE.
PS8647.O622T464 2013   jC813'.6   C2012-908289-9

Kids Can Press is a *lorus*™ Entertainment company

TEN BIRDS
Meet a Monster

Cybèle Young

KIDS CAN PRESS

TEN birds came
across a scary monster.
What were they to do?

The first bird, always inventive,

became a *Vicious Polka-dactyl*.

But the monster didn't budge.

The second bird, always resourceful, joined in.

Together they became a *Gnashing Grapplesaurus*.

But the monster didn't move a muscle.

The third bird, always a hard worker, joined in.

Together they became a *Frightening Vipper-Snapper*.

But the monster wasn't fazed.

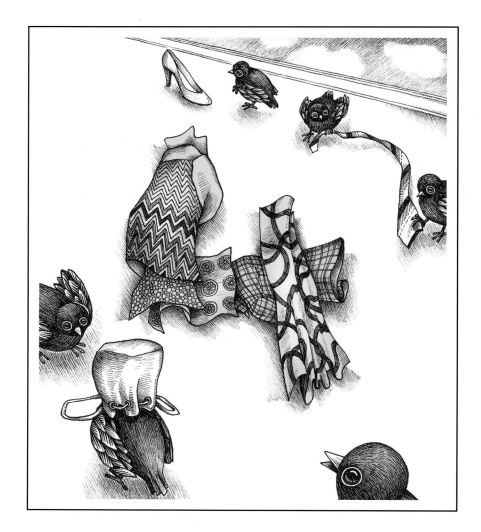

The fourth bird, always attentive, joined in.

Together they became a *Scaly Triple-Claw*.

But the monster stayed put.

The fifth bird, always diligent, joined in.

Together they became a *Bristling Fang-Mangler*.

But the monster didn't seem to care.

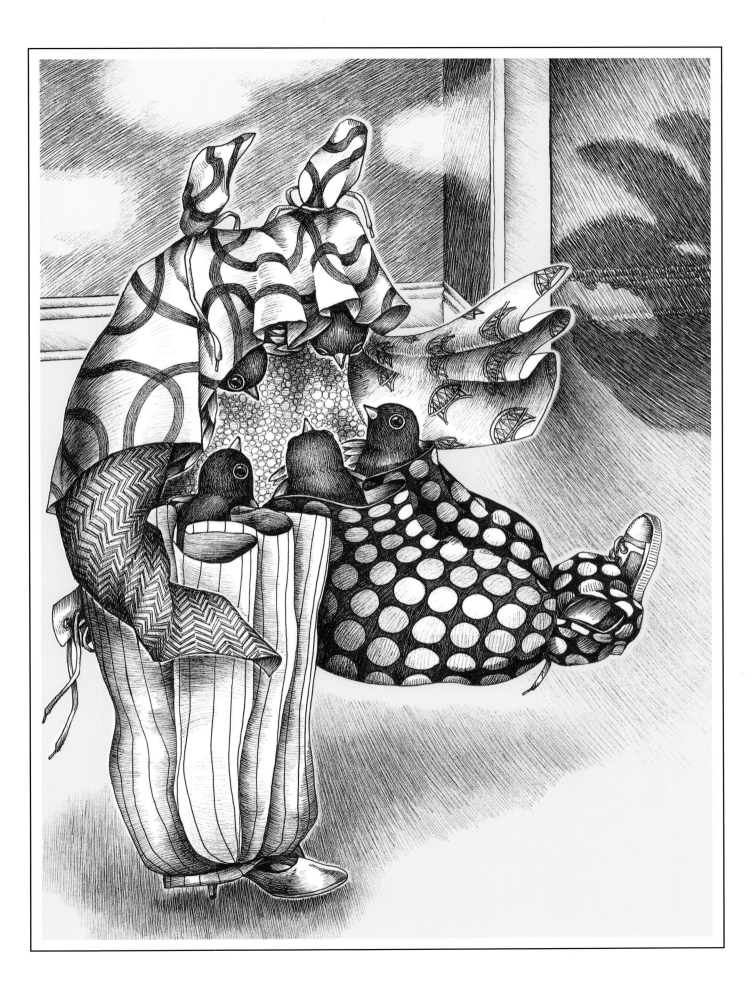

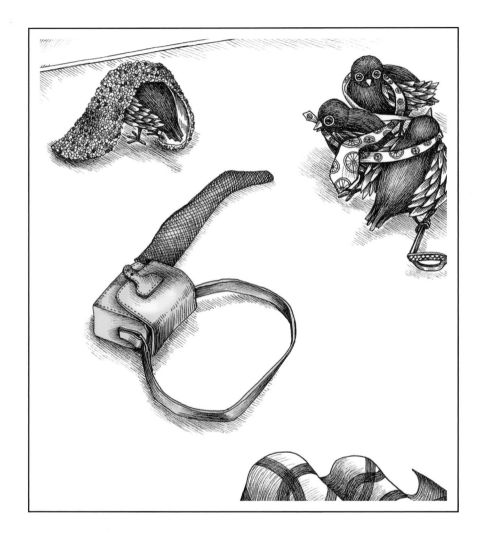

The sixth bird, always creative, joined in.

Together they became a *Horrific Hooded-Smasher*.

But the monster remained indifferent.

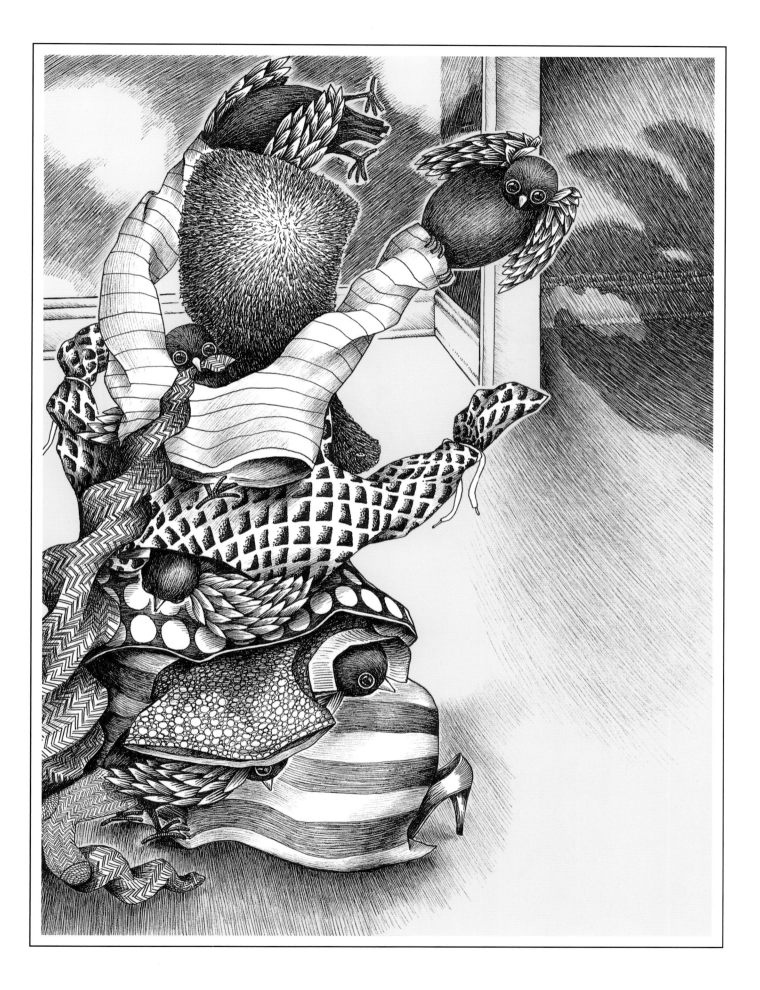

The seventh bird, always eager to participate, joined in.
Together they became a *Terrifying Crackatoothus*.
But the monster ignored it.

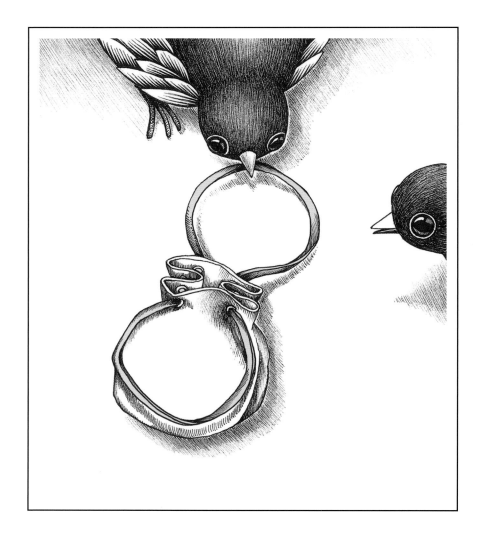

The eighth bird, always a team player, joined in.
Together they became a *Slimy Long-toed Zapper*.
But the monster was unmoved.

The ninth bird, always imaginative, joined in.

Together they became a *Hideous Whip-tail Gangle Raptor*.

The monster stood its ground.

But – the tenth bird, always easily distracted,
began to wander around ...

… and he happened to find
just the right thing.